Cont...

Chapter 1
The Best Day of My Life

It's always horrible when you start at a new school.

It's even worse when you have to start in Spring. By Spring, everyone has made all their new mates. Then up pops a new boy, and no one wants to know.

Today I was that new boy. Ben the new boy, on his first day in school.

I had to wait outside the Head's office first thing. He wanted to have a few words with me. Yawn!

I was feeling funny as I sat there. For the first time ever I was wearing contact lenses, not glasses. And I'd had my hair cut short. I was glad no one was looking at me.

And then someone was.

It was a girl.

A stunning girl, looking right at me.

Then the girl walked over to me. I hoped my face wasn't bright red. At least she couldn't hear my heart thumping away.

"Hi," she said. "You're new, aren't you?"

"Yeah," I mumbled. "I'm Ben."

The girl gave a funny little gasp. "Does your other name begin with an 'M'?" she asked.

'What an odd question,' I thought. But I was happy to answer any silly question this dream girl asked. And she was right. My second name did begin with an 'M'.

"How did you know that?" I asked.

She just giggled.

Then the Head came out of his office.

"Why aren't you in class?" he snapped at the girl.

"I'm just going, Sir," she said.

She smiled back at me as she turned to walk away. "I'm Jasmine," she whispered. "See you, Awesome!"

Wow. I take back anything I said about being the new boy. Today was the best day of my life. The most beautiful girl I'd ever seen had just called me 'awesome'.

I should have dumped my glasses years ago.

Without them it seems I'm a total girl magnet!

Chapter 2
A Big Secret

Jasmine wasn't in my class or any of my lessons that morning. I wondered when I'd see her again.

A boy called Ty had been told to look after me. I asked him about Jasmine as we walked to the dinner hall for lunch.

Ty groaned. "Every guy in school fancies her. But she turns us all down. She doesn't think any of us are good enough."

Then he stopped. His eyes opened wide with amazement. Jasmine was sitting in the dinner hall, waiting for us. Well, for me, I suppose. She waved when she saw us.

"Hi," she called. "How's it going? Sit with me!"

We sat down beside her and ate our lunches. She was super friendly the whole time. Then Ty had to go off to play football. Jasmine stayed with me.

To tell the truth, she didn't say much. She just smiled.

'She must really like me,' I thought.

Then her mobile rang. The ring tone was so loud it made me jump.

"Can't talk now," Jasmine snapped at the person on the phone. She rang off and turned back to me.

"My ring tone really made you jump," she said. She gave an odd smile. "Do you remember what show it's from?"

I didn't, and then I did. It was from a TV series called 'Awesome'.

'Awesome' was about a boy who was always in trouble, often with girls. And any time a girl asked his name, he'd say, "Hey, just call me 'Awesome'."

That's just what Jasmine had called me.

Even with my glasses on, people had told me I looked a bit like the actor who played Awesome. The actor's name was Ben too. Ben Moore. My name is Ben MacBean.

"It's a shame 'Awesome' stopped," Jasmine said.

"Yeah," I agreed.

"Ben Moore gave it all up, didn't he?" said Jasmine. "Two years ago. I wonder why?" She turned to me as if I'd know. I hadn't a clue. I tried to think of something.

"Maybe he'd had enough of show business," I said. "Maybe he wanted to concentrate on keeping it real."

"Yeah, could be," said Jasmine with a nod. "But we'll never know as he doesn't even tweet. He's just disappeared."

Jasmine was looking right at me now, and she had a funny look on her face. "He's still my favourite actor in the whole world," she said. "I'd give anything to meet him."

So now I knew why Jasmine had been so nice to me. She thought I was Ben Moore.

Of course, I knew I wasn't.

I knew I should tell her the truth. But she was so beautiful, and I was having such a great time. So I decided to wait until the next day.

The next day Jasmine followed me everywhere. Ty and the other boys in my class all noticed. "You're well in there," said Ty. He sounded jealous.

After school, Jasmine insisted on walking home with me. When we stopped at my gate, she got all serious.

"I know you want to be private," she whispered. "You don't want anyone to guess your secret identity. But you're not really Ben MacBean, are you?"

"I'm not?" I asked.

She laughed. "I bet no one in the world is called MacBean."

Well ... I was, for one. But I didn't say anything.

"You ARE him, aren't you?" she said.

"Who?" I asked.

"Ben Moore," she whispered.

I know what I should have said. I should have said, "No, I am not Ben Moore. I'm Ben MacBean. I just happen to look a bit like Ben Moore." In fact, I almost did say it. But Jasmine was so excited. And I couldn't let her down, could I? So instead I whispered, "I never talk about that ..."

She broke in. "I understand," she said. "But you are Ben Moore, aren't you?"

I took a deep breath and hissed. "All right, you've found me out."

I thought Jasmine was going to faint with joy.

"But you will never, ever tell anyone, will you?" I said.

"Never!" said Jasmine. "I promise. But it's amazing that you've come here. I mean, you're a total legend. I had pictures of you all over my bedroom wall."

I blushed.

"You were so mint in 'Awesome'," she went on. "Why did you give it all up?"

"Well, I ..."

"In your last ever interview you said everything was getting mad. You wanted to get your life back again."

"Yeah, that's it," I agreed, pleased that she seemed to be able to answer all her questions for me. "I wanted to go back to being normal."

"I read you had gone back to school somewhere quiet," she gushed. "But I never dreamt it would be at my school! This is just so, so ..." she gulped. "I'd better go now before

I say something totally embarrassing. Bye, Awesome!"

I stared after her. Then I noticed Mum watching us from the kitchen window. I waved and went in.

"Making friends already?" Mum asked.

"Yeah," I said.

"She looks like a nice girl."

"She is."

"I think she likes you." Mum smiled, to tease me.

"I wish she did," I said.

And I did wish it. But I knew Jasmine didn't really like me. She liked the boy off her favourite TV show.

It wasn't fair to lead her on. I had to tell her the truth. As soon as I did that, she'd ignore me forever.

So that's why I decided to keep pretending a bit longer – and ask Jasmine to go out with me.

Chapter 3
My Fan Club

All evening I Googled stuff about Ben Moore.
I went on YouTube and watched some old
episodes of 'Awesome'. Then I went up to my
bedroom and copied how he moved.

Next day I strolled into school just like Ben
Moore. A girl in my class called Chloe rushed

up to me. She whispered something so low that I couldn't hear.

"What did you say?" I asked.

"I'll never tell," she hissed.

"Never tell what?"

"I know who you really are," she said. "So could I just have your autograph? I think you're proper cool."

I looked around, scared that someone would have heard. Luckily no one seemed to be watching. I'd Googled Ben Moore's autograph last night, so I was able to copy it.

"Don't let anyone else see this," I whispered, when it was done.

"Oh don't worry, I won't," she promised. "And I won't try and sell your autograph on eBay either."

I was really cross Jasmine had given away my secret identity. Later on, I confronted her about it. "But Chloe's my very best friend," she explained. I tell her everything. And she's promised she won't tell another person."

Jasmine was in a dead good mood. After a while, I calmed down too. Perhaps it would all be all right.

That night I was Googling more facts about Ben Moore when Mum called me downstairs.

"There are four girls hanging about outside. And they all want to see you."

"Me?" I was amazed.

"Yes, you," said Mum.

When I stepped outside three of the girls started to clap and cheer. The other one just seemed very embarrassed. That was Chloe.

"I'm so sorry," she hissed. "I told my little sister in total confidence about your secret identity. She's only gone and blabbed it to our cousins ..."

"My name's Rosie," one of the other girls broke in. "And we all thought you were so amazing on that show. We even had your calendar. I wish we still had it, but Mum put it out for recycling. You're on a mouse mat as well, aren't you?"

"Yeah, I am," I said, with a proud grin.

"I'd love to have my face on a mouse mat," said Rosie. "It would be such an honour."

"And you painted a picture for charity, didn't you?" said another girl.

"Er, two pictures, actually," I said. I knew more about Ben Moore than his own mum by now.

It was sort of fun signing the autographs and listening to them tell me how great I was. But after a while I sent them home.

"Please don't tell anyone else," I said. "I just want to forget my days as a top star now."

Back inside Mum was dying to find out what was going on. "It was like your fan club out there," she said.

"Yeah, I do seem to have become a bit popular, don't I?"

The next day, Ty asked me if I was really Awesome off the telly.

I just said, "I don't want to talk about it."

How on earth had he found out?

"Fair enough," he said. "But you are, aren't you?"

"Yeah, but please don't tell anyone," I said, in the end.

"You know what, I always hated that show," said Ty. "And I thought you were rubbish on it."

Ty ignored me for the rest of the day. But he was the only one.

All over the school people were taking pictures of me on their mobiles. And I signed loads more autographs. One was for a teacher, only she snapped, "Please understand it's for my niece, not me."

Then this girl came up to me and started to feel my nose.

"Hey, what are you doing?" I shouted, as I fought her off.

"I wanted to see if you'd got a new nose," she said. "Someone said on ..."

"I haven't!" I interrupted, cross. "It's all mine."

Jasmine walked home with me again.

"Everyone at school knows," I said.

"I can't understand how that happened," she said. "I only told Chloe, but now ..." She sneaked a look at me. "Are you very angry?"

"Furious," I said. "But I'll forgive you ... if you go out with me on Saturday night."

Jasmine's eyes opened wide. "If I say yes, it's not because you're a famous person. I would have said yes anyway."

"Thanks for that," I said.

"I mean it," she said.

We made a date to go to the cinema the next night.

I was so happy and excited – until another load of girls turned up outside my house, wanting autographs.

"What's going on?" Mum demanded. "Why do all those girls want your autograph?"

"They just like me, I guess," I said.

"One of them even asked me for my autograph," said Mum.

"They must like you too," I said. "We're just a really popular family. It'll calm down soon – I hope."

Then I added. "By the way, Mum, I'm going out on a date tomorrow with Jasmine."

"That's the pretty girl who walked home with you."

"The very same," I said. And I couldn't help smiling.

I really was living the dream – even if it was someone else's dream. I'd just borrowed it off Ben Moore for a while.

But then my mobile rang. It was Jasmine. "I so wish you'd told me ..." she began.

"Told you what?" I asked.

"I suppose our date is off tomorrow," she said. "Well, you can't be in two places at once."

I was totally lost. "Jasmine, what are you talking about?"

She sniffed. "It's all over the internet. You're breaking your silence, and giving a 30 minute interview live on webcam tomorrow night."

Chapter 4
The Worst Disaster Ever

I was so shocked I couldn't think what to
say.

"So what made you change your mind?"
Jasmine asked. She still sounded sniffly.

I hadn't a clue what to say, but I had to
think of something, and fast. In the end I said,

"Well, I really care about my fans. I thought I owed it to them to say something."

"Will you be talking to them from your house?" she asked.

"Er ... yeah. That's where I'll be talking to them from," I said. "The very place."

"I could be there too, if you like," said Jasmine. "As ... your new girlfriend." Her voice rose with excitement. "One TV star and his girlfriend went out and got matching tattoos. We could do that if you like. Or maybe we could just wear matching outfits."

"I'd love that," I said. "But I'm not sure my fans would like it."

"That's true," she said. "They'd all be so jealous of me."

"Tell you what, we'll still go to the cinema when I've finished," I said. "I'm not missing that."

When I hung up the phone I was shaking. Now what was I going to do? Pretend I was talking to everyone from my house? But how could I get away with that?

The next day was Saturday. In the morning I pulled back the curtains to see more girls waiting outside the house. I rushed downstairs before Mum could speak to them. They all wanted to know why I was breaking my silence. So I explained again how I was doing it for my fans. But I was getting sick of this. It was turning into the worst disaster ever.

"I've spoke to some of those girls outside," Mum said when I got back in. "They called me Mrs Moore."

"They're having a joke with you," I said.

"But why would they do that?" asked Mum. "And why are they calling you Ben Moore?" Then she stopped. "Isn't there an actor called Ben Moore?"

"My double," I muttered.

Then I told her everything. It was a relief actually.

Afterwards Mum said, "When I was a girl I used to run round the playground pretending to be Wonder Woman. It was fun, for a little while. Did you really think you'd get away with this?"

"Well, I nearly did," I said. "Until the real Ben Moore announced he was giving an interview. He's messed up everything."

"It's time to tell people the truth," said Mum. "Starting with Jasmine."

I agreed. I nearly sent her a text, but in the end I decided that only a coward would do that. I would have to explain face-to-face, but I'd wait until after Ben Moore's interview. Jasmine would have found out the truth by then anyway. I'd just say I was really sorry and I still hoped she'd go out with me.

Some hope!

The Ben Moore interview went out at 6pm. I couldn't bear to watch it. I was sick of him. At 6.30, I walked over to Jasmine's house.

"Good luck," called Mum.

"Thanks," I called back. "I'll need it."

Chapter 5
Messing Everything Up

Jasmine was upstairs with Chloe. They were both sitting at her computer screen. They both looked at me hard as I walked in.

"Why did you do it?" Jasmine asked.

"Good question," I said. "Look, I never meant to pretend to be Awesome. It just happened and ..."

I tailed off. Jasmine's mouth had fallen open and she looked totally shocked.

"You're not Awesome?" she gasped.

"No! I thought you'd have guessed," I said. "I mean, you saw the web chat."

Chloe stood up. "You – I mean Ben Moore – cancelled the web chat at the last minute."

"We were just asking you why you cancelled it," added Jasmine. "So, why did you pretend to be Ben Moore when you're not?" She sounded very hurt and upset.

"Because you wanted me to be Ben Moore so much," I said. "And I didn't want to disappoint you."

"So you lied," she snapped.

"No, not lied ... I pretended. And that's different – in a way. And now I've come to ask if you still want to go to the cinema with me."

"You've got a nerve," cried Chloe.

"No I haven't, because Jasmine said she'd go out with me even if I wasn't him."

"But that was when she thought you were famous," said Chloe. "She thought you were someone."

"I am someone," I said. "I'm me. Ben MacBean. So will you go out with me, Jasmine?"

Jasmine turned away from me. "Just get out," she said.

"You heard her!" shouted Chloe.

I closed the door behind me and turned for home.

When people at school found out I wasn't really Ben Moore – well, I didn't even want to think about that. It would be horrible. They'd really feel I'd let them down.

But none of that mattered. Not really. What mattered was that I'd lost Jasmine. She'd probably never talk to me again.

And then I heard footsteps.

I stopped. Jasmine was running towards me. She looked ... she looked furious.

"I'm so angry with you, Ben," she shouted. "I suppose you really are called Ben?"

"Yeah, that bit is true. Honest."

"But I'm also ..." She stopped to get her breath.

"Yes?" I said.

"Well, I do sort of like you. Oh, I'm all mixed up."

"Sorry, but I ..." I began.

"Shut up for a second," she said.

"Anything you say."

"Tell me this, Ben MacBean ..."

I looked at her. "I'll tell you anything you want to know."

"Are we too late for the cinema?"

I smiled. "Not if we run."

"Well, come on then," said Jasmine. "Let's run."

Our books are tested
for children and young people by
children and young people.

Thanks to everyone who consulted on
a manuscript for their time and effort in
helping us to make our books better
for our readers.

"But I mealso ..." She stopped to get her breath.

"Yes?" I said.

"Well, I do sort of like you. Oh, I'm all mixed up ..."

"Sorry, but I ..." I began.

"Shut up for a second," she said.

"Anything you say."

"Tell me this, Ben MacBean ..."